★ PAWTRIOT ★
DOGS
ON THE FREEDOM TRAIL

★ PAWTRIOT ★
DOGS

ON THE FREEDOM TRAIL

by Samuel P. Fortsch
illustrated by Manuel Gutierrez

GROSSET & DUNLAP

GROSSET & DUNLAP
An Imprint of Penguin Random House LLC, New York

Photo credit: cover: (paper background): darkbird77/iStock/Getty Images Plus

Visit us online at www.penguinrandomhouse.com.

Library of Congress Control Number: 2020024879

ISBN 9780593222362   10 9 8 7 6 5 4 3 2 1

I dedicate this book to the brave men and women
of the US Armed Forces. And to my editor for
his endless patience and hard work—SPF

In memory of Copito, Colita, Toby, Nuky, Flavor, Hermes,
Orson, Jay Boy, and John Fitzgerald Tinta—MG

CHAPTER 1
LAND HO!

Location: USS *George Washington*, Atlantic
        Ocean
Date: 20MAR21
Time: 1100 hours

Welcome back on board, soldier!

Our time on the USS *George Washington*, the United States Navy's premier nuclear-powered aircraft carrier, is coming to an end. Today's the day we dock in Boston! We've been on the ship for three days, making our way up the Atlantic coast from the Caribbean. This massive ship is as big as it is slow. We're lumbering through the ocean at a top speed of about twenty-six knots—that's only thirty miles per hour.

Now that we're getting close to Boston Harbor, here's a quick debrief to get you caught up to speed.

After we battled long and hard against the Thrice-Cursed Pirate Sea Wolf and his vicious crew, the Cutthroats, the Pawtriots and I were finally able to get some much-needed *R&R*—that's Army-talk for "rest and relaxation."

And trust me, after our last mission, it was much needed.

Our fight against the pirates was dangerous and full of peril, but the Pawtriots banded together and never lost hope.

We even added two more Pawtriots to our ranks: twin beagles named Jag and Jet. Jag is in the Navy. He's a by-the-book hard-liner who never breaks the rules, except for that one time when he commandeered a ship to save my tail and his sister's, too. Jet, his sister, is a hard-charging Coast Guard dog who is more than willing to bend the rules. They received special exemptions to help the Pawtriots on all future missions. They're both welcome additions to the Pawtriots' ranks!

All this downtime aboard the USS *George Washington* has really let us bond as a unit. Aside from the occasional argument between Brick and Franny, things are going great.

I've even been able to do roll call every morning

at 0630 sharp to make sure everyone is present and accounted for.

After roll call, I lead the Pawtriots in *PT.* That's Army-talk for "physical training." To keep us fit while on board this ship, we do a lot of exercises, sprints, and, of course, *paw*-ups! We're going to need to be in tip-top

Lindy
Jet
Jag
Brick
Franny
Smithers
Penny
Simon
Daisy
& Puppies

shape for our long march down to Washington, DC. Once we dock in Boston, we have a seven-hundred-klick trek. *Klick* is Army-talk for "kilometer." Our plan is to hitch as many rides as we can, but the Pawtriots need to be prepared for anything because sometimes even the best-laid plans can go wrong. When I was in the Army, our platoon sergeant always had a plan for when things went wrong. A good leader always prepares for the worst but hopes for the best.

The sun is shining, the sky is blue, and there isn't a cloud in the sky. I watch as sailors race across the deck with smiles stretched across their faces. I realize that we're not the only ones who are excited to get off this ship.

I look out at Boston Harbor. I see a beautiful city filled with glass-and-steel buildings that pierce the sky. The docks are full of cheering families waving American flags. They're ready to welcome home loved ones who have been far from home for a very long time.

I gathered all the Pawtriots on deck, so we could soak in this powerful moment together as a unit. I know the people aren't waving and cheering for the Pawtriots, but, in a way, it almost seems like they are, and that makes me feel good inside. It makes me feel proud to be an American.

We all wait with eager anticipation as the massive ship slows down and carefully begins to dock.

"Have any of you ever been to Boston?" asks Jag.

"Negative," I say as the rest of the Pawtriots, except Jet, shake their heads side to side, signaling "no."

"I've been here a bunch of times," says Jet. "I love the food here, and I know a ton of great spots to eat. And this city is full of history, too."

"Like what?" Brick asks.

"The American Revolution began just a short eleven miles northwest of here, in Lexington, Massachusetts, on April nineteenth, 1775," says Jet. "You should know that. Aren't you British?"

"*Oi!* Of course I know that. I'm just a little fuzzy on the details," Brick says.

"Ssso," Smithers begins, "Bossston wasss crucial during the War of Independence. The colonialsss and the Britisssh fought hard to sssecure thisss ssstrategic ssstronghold."

Smithers continues retelling a bit of history and I begin drifting off a bit, remembering when my old Army handler, Kris, used to tell me all her favorite moments of American history. She loved the American Revolution and reciting stories from it, such as the Battle of Bunker Hill in 1775, when the American colonial troops were vastly outnumbered by British troops. Kris told me it was a fierce battle that happened right here in Boston!

I snap out of my daydream and turn to Smithers. "I didn't know you were such a history buff, Smithers!"

"Why, I sssuppossse I am!" says Smithers.

"*Oi!* Enough with these old-timey stories. I'm hungry! Take me to the food, Jet!" Brick says, and everyone laughs. I'm glad to see my unit in good spirits before we make our long trek back home. A happy unit is a motivated unit. And we're going to need all the motivation we can get.

I turn to the group. "Listen up, Pawtriots. I wish we had more time to explore this city. I love history and good food, but we're on a mission to get back home . . . and quickly. Morgan and Sawyer are back at the TOC and we're their reinforcements. Are you all tracking?" I say.

"Tracking," all of the Pawtriots say in unison.

"Good. The ship is about to finish docking in Boston Harbor. In a few minutes we'll be getting off. Once we're on dry land, we'll get some hot chow in our bellies and then head south."

Location: Docks, Boston Harbor
Time: 1400 hours

"*Oi!* Rico, what's going on? I'm starving here, and you said we'd be off the ship an hour ago," Brick hollers.

"At ease, Brick. It shouldn't be much longer," I say.

"Tell that to my stomach," Brick fires back.

I don't know what the holdup is, but the sailors haven't let anyone off the ship. I'm beginning to think something might be wrong, but I don't want to worry my unit if I don't know all the details myself.

"Just try to relax," I tell Brick.

I let my mind wander as I stare off at Boston Harbor. Then my daze is suddenly interrupted. I look up and see a seagull flying right toward me.

I quickly step back as the seagull practically crashes at my feet. She's exhausted, so I help her to her feet and notice a folded-up piece of paper in her beak.

"Are you Sergeant Rico?" she asks, handing the paper to me.

"Yes ma'am," I say.

"I've got an urgent Situation Report from your Pawtriot friends at the TOC," she says. "I haven't stopped flying since they gave it to me."

I unfold the message as the rest of the Pawtriots gather around me while the seagull catches her breath.

"It's from Morgan and Sawyer," I say.

"Who are they?" asks Jet.

"They're our rabbit and ferret friends in

Washington, DC. I left them in charge of the TOC when we left for our mission in Texas," I say.

"Do you have anything to report back to your friends at the TOC?" she asks.

"Tell them help is on the way," I say as I salute the seagull and watch her fly away.

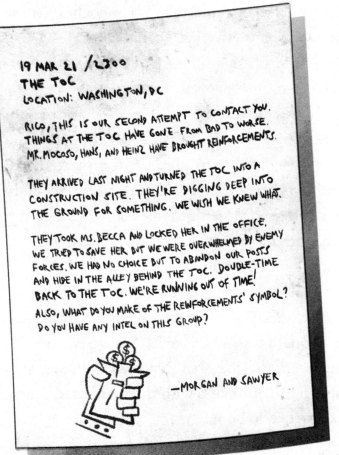

19 MAR 21 /2300
THE TOC
LOCATION: WASHINGTON, DC

RICO, THIS IS OUR SECOND ATTEMPT TO CONTACT YOU.
THINGS AT THE TOC HAVE GONE FROM BAD TO WORSE.
MR. MOCOSO, HANS, AND HEINZ HAVE BROUGHT REINFORCEMENTS.

THEY ARRIVED LAST NIGHT AND TURNED THE TOC INTO A
CONSTRUCTION SITE. THEY'RE DIGGING DEEP INTO
THE GROUND FOR SOMETHING. WE WISH WE KNEW WHAT.

THEY TOOK MS. BECCA AND LOCKED HER IN THE OFFICE.
WE TRIED TO SAVE HER BUT WE WERE OVERWHELMED BY ENEMY
FORCES. WE HAD NO CHOICE BUT TO ABANDON OUR POSTS
AND HIDE IN THE ALLEY BEHIND THE TOC. DOUBLE-TIME
BACK TO THE TOC. WE'RE RUNNING OUT OF TIME!
ALSO, WHAT DO YOU MAKE OF THE REINFORCEMENTS' SYMBOL?
DO YOU HAVE ANY INTEL ON THIS GROUP?

—MORGAN AND SAWYER

I don't know what to make of the mysterious symbol. All I know is that Mr. Mocoso and his nasty Doberman pinschers, Hans and Heinz, are plotting something evil at our home base. I thought after we stopped them the first time that they would have learned their lesson. Clearly, I was wrong. Some people and their pooches just never know when they've been conquered.

I hold up the SitRep and point at the strange symbol so the Pawtriots can see.

"Does anyone recognize this?" I ask the unit. I watch as all the Pawtriots look at the symbol.

As I continue to hold up the piece of paper, Smithers slithers forward and wraps around my body to get a closer look.

"Asss a matter of fact, I sssupossse I do know that sssymbol," Smithers says.

"What does it mean?" I ask.

"It meansss we're in far more trouble than previousssly sssusssspected," Smithers says. "It'sss the mark of the Red Handsss. They're an evil bunch of criminalsss with three hundred yearsss of experience to boot."

"We've battled far worse," says Franny.

Franny's right. We battled the Beast, a massive crocodile down in the sewers of Washington, DC; the Eight-Legged Killer, a nuclear spider in an abandoned mine shaft in Texas; and even the Kraken, a gigantic and ferocious squid living in a blue lagoon inside the island's Crystal Caves.

Every mission the Pawtriots have set out to accomplish has had its series of challenges. I know this mission will be no different.

"Smithers, what else can you tell us about the Red Hands?" I ask.

"Sssecrecy isss their modusss operandi. That'sss Latin for 'mode of operation.' The Red Handsss have been ssstealing treasssure for centuriesss. They usssed to have horsssesss and wooden ssshipsss. Now they have fancy tanksss and helicoptersss. They ussse their ssstolen treasssure for evil. And you can bet your tail that they'll have sssomething sssinisssster planned for usss once we return to the TOC," says Smithers.

"Failure isn't an option. Our friends are in serious trouble," says Penny.

"The Pawtriots don't back down from a fight. *Hooah?*" I ask.

"*Hooah!*" shout the Pawtriots.

Our simple mission might have gotten a little more complex, but that doesn't change a thing. Once we get off this ship, we'll head straight to the TOC in Washington, DC.

CHAPTER 2
LOCKDOWN

Location: Docks, USS *George Washington*
Time: 1500 hours

We make our way across the deck toward the front of the ship and form up next to all the sailors. They're smiling and talking about how excited they are to be reunited with their families. I watch as a massive loading ramp is lowered onto the deck of the ship so the sailors can walk off.

As I scan the area I notice an old rottweiler standing by himself toward the back of the deck. I can tell just by looking at him that he's a US marine. He's wearing a tan combat vest and looks like he hasn't smiled in weeks.

"Hang tight, Pawtriots. I'm going to go say hello to this rottweiler," I say.

But suddenly there's a commotion near the front of the line. I can hear some of the older

sailors shouting orders as the younger sailors start grumbling.

I get worried as the sailors' smiles quickly turn into frowns.

"What's going on, Rico?" asks Penny as the crowd of sailors starts shuffling back toward us.

"I don't know, just stick together," I say.

I look around, and the chaos of the situation seems to be getting worse by the second. Sailors are racing around the deck, setting up barriers in front of the loading ramp to make sure no one can leave.

I'm not sure what's happening, but I'm hoping

Jet and Jag can gather some intel for us.

"Jet, Jag. Go see if you can figure out what's going on," I shout over the noise.

"Tracking. We'll be right back," says Jag as he races off with Jet.

It's been thirty mikes since I sent Jet and Jag to gather intel. I'm anxious to hear what they found out.

Here they come now.

"What do you have to report?" I ask them.

"They initiated this lockdown for safety reasons. A 'protective measure' is the term they used," says Jag.

"Protection from what?" I ask.

"Oh, you know, just some super-secret weapon and an entire battalion of corgis is all," Jet says with a hint of sarcasm.

"Like the British dogs?" Penny asks.

"Close. Corgis are Welsh, actually. Wales is part

of the United Kingdom," says Franny.

Jag chimes in, "Affirmative. Despite her sarcasm, I'm afraid Jet's serious. And one of the sailors showed us a picture of the corgis to prove it. What is even more strange is that the same mysterious symbol from the SitRep is on their combat vests."

"I guess Smithers was right," I say.

"The Red Handsss musssst be in Bossston, and I'd bet they're waiting for usss," Smithers says.

"What do they want with us?" Penny asks.

"I don't know. But we have to get off this ship," I say.

"Negative. They won't let anyone leave for forty-eight hours," Jag says.

"That's two days!" Penny shouts as she turns to look at me. "Rico, we can't wait that long."

Penny's right. Forty-eight hours is far too long. We don't have time to waste—we need to get back to the TOC. I must think of a plan and quickly.

I know sneaking off is against protocol, but it's our only option. It won't be easy to sneak off, especially all of us at the same time, but I think I have a plan and I *know* Penny won't like it.

"Penny, cover your ears," I say.

"Why?" she says.

"Because we're splitting up," I say.

"Ugh. Rico, you know I hate splitting up! What's your plan this time?" Penny asks.

"We'll have two teams: Alpha and Bravo. Alpha team will be in charge of sneaking everyone off this ship. Penny, I want you to be team leader for Alpha, tracking?"

"Tracking," says Penny as she renders a crisp salute.

"On Alpha team will be Brick, Franny, Smithers, Simon, Daisy, the puppies, Lindy, Jet, and Jag."

I feel confident having Penny lead Alpha team. I'd follow her anywhere, and I know every other Pawtriot would, too. She's smart as a whip, makes quick decisions, and doesn't crack under pressure. Those are traits every good leader needs.

I look over and notice Penny doing the "tilt" as she counts the names of Alpha team on her paws.

"Wait. That's everyone but you," Penny says.

"That's right. I'm Bravo team. There are too many of us to sneak out all at once. So I'm going to create a diversion. *Hooah?*" I ask.

"*Hooah!*" the Pawtriots say in unison.

"I'll draw everyone's attention away from you. Once the sailors are distracted, I want you all to exfil over that barrier and sprint down that loading ramp. Don't look back; just keep moving. Can I get a *north south*?" I ask.

The Pawtriots all nod their heads up and down in agreement as I continue, effectively giving me a *north south*.

"And then find a safe place to hide," I say.

"I know just the spot," says Jet. "It's called the Green Dragon Tavern, and it was nicknamed the 'Headquarters of the Revolution' by historians. The Sons of Liberty, who were a secret organization of American colonists fighting taxation by the British government, met at the Green Dragon Tavern every night and plotted the Boston Tea Party from there!"

"That'sss absssolutely correct," Smithers says.

"Sounds like a great plan. I'll meet you there as soon as I can get off this ship," I say.

I'm hoping the sailors guarding the perimeter

will focus all their attention on me and won't notice the rest of the Pawtriots sneaking off. I'll only have one shot at this, so I need to make it count.

I make my way into the middle of a group of sailors and start barking as loudly as I can. But with all the commotion, no one really seems to notice.

I need to up the ante.

I quickly scan the area to see if there's something I can knock over that might cause a loud bang—a distraction. Then I see the rottweiler from earlier walking toward Penny and the rest of Alpha team. I worry he might blow Alpha team's escape, but then I have an idea.

Without thinking it through, I begin weaving in and out of the crowd through sailors' legs, making my way right for the rottweiler.

Once I have a clear path, I gather up a full head of steam and run top speed, my wheel below me spinning as fast as possible.

Wham!

I make direct contact with the rottweiler, sending us both off our feet and onto the ground.

"What is your major malfunction?!" the rottweiler shouts as he staggers to his feet.

"I'm sorry. I wasn't paying attention to where I was going," I say.

"It's too late for apologies, you slime sucker. The damage is already done," he says, walking right toward me with his chest puffed out.

With each passing second, I can see the marine is getting angrier and angrier. He brings his snout right up to my snout. My impromptu plan is working just like I hoped. Now I need to send him over the edge.

"I knew you Army dogs weren't the brightest," he says.

"Coming from a Devil Dog, I'll take that as a compliment," I say as the rottweiler shows his teeth and menacing grin.

"You better not be making any sort of negative inference about my beloved Marine Corps!"

I can tell he's about to lose his cool with me. So I open my mouth to show him my teeth and make it clear that I'm not scared or ready to back down. I let out a growl so he knows I'm ready, and he suddenly lunges right for me, sending me crashing down hard onto my side.

CHAPTER 3
OVERBOARD

Location: Deck, USS *George Washington*
Time: 1845 hours

Well, my plan worked—sort of. I created a distraction that allowed Alpha team to escape. But my distraction also caught the attention of the Master-at-Arms—that's the person in charge of enforcing the law for the Navy.

The Master-at-Arms wasn't a huge fan of my little sideshow, so he put the marine and me on leashes and tied us to the railing that runs along the deck of the ship. He even put some sailors in charge of guarding us. We've been here for at least three hours or so. I've noticed the guards have been taking one-hour shifts watching over us before switching.

During their shift changes, I've been quietly biting, scratching, and clawing through my leash so that when the time comes, I can escape and link up with the rest of the Pawtriots at the Green Dragon Tavern.

"Give it a rest, would you?" says the marine as I continue gnawing at my leash.

"Negative, we have to get out of here," I say.

"*We?* There is no *we*. And besides, I already know Boston like the back of my paw. I got no plans to go sightseeing today," he says.

"I don't want to sightsee, either," I say to him. "My unit is in trouble, so I need to get off this ship. My name's Sergeant Rico and my unit is the Pawtriots. What's your name and rank?"

"Listen, pal. I'm not in the mood to talk, especially to some Army dog who got me leashed up for insubordination," the rottweiler says.

"I already told you, I'm sorry. But I had to do it to help my unit escape. I needed a distraction, and, well, you were the perfect distraction," I plead with him.

"And I told you, I don't care about you or your unit. Today's my last day in the Corps, and I most certainly didn't plan on spending it tied up with you. So how about you keep your Army nose out of my Marine Corps business until we're released? They'll let us loose in the morning," he says.

"I don't have until the morning. I received this SitRep from a carrier seagull earlier today," I say as I slide the paper to him.

He picks it up with his paw. He begins reading the SitRep and I can see his eyes grow wide.

"You recognize that symbol, don't you?" I ask him.

"Roger that. Unfortunately, I do," he says.

"So you know my unit's in serious trouble and we need help, right?" I say.

"You don't want my help. I'm not the marine I used to be. I'm getting forced out. 'Medically discharged' is what they said. I'm too old and too slow. I can't keep up anymore," he says.

"Trust me, I know *exactly* what it's like," I say, pointing to my leg. "Is there any intel you can give me about them?"

"Well," he begins to say, but then stops. I can tell he's hesitant to share any information with a perfect stranger.

"I'm former Army and you're a marine. We might not be in the same unit, but we're on the same team," I remind him.

He takes a deep breath.

"It wasn't too long ago—maybe nine months—I was with my unit overseas. We were on a peacekeeping mission, but you can never be too careful. I was in charge of clearing the roads of any booby traps or bad guys."

"So what happened?" I ask.

"Everything was going according to plan. We were marching toward a village to link up with locals to provide them with medical supplies and food. The sun had been beating down on us all day. I was burning up and getting tired, but I didn't want to quit. I kept pushing and pushing until I collapsed to the ground. My unit kept marching forward without me," he says.

He takes another deep breath. I can see this is a hard story for him to tell.

"And that's when I saw the explosion. *Boom!*" he says. "I got up and just started sprinting forward to help my unit. But by the time I got there, it was too late. The Red Hands had set a trap for my unit and me, and I failed to stop it. I'll never forgive myself," he says, wiping a single tear off his face with his paw.

"You can't blame yourself," I say. "Look at me: I lost my military bearing chasing what I thought was a piece of bacon. And it cost me my leg. And I never saw my handler, Kris, after the explosion," I tell him.

"That must be hard to deal with, too," the rottweiler says.

"It is, but you have to keep going. Just know I've been exactly where you are. Everyone around you is saying you can't do anything anymore, but that's not true. I've wanted to give up on myself. And maybe you do, too, right now. But you're a marine. And once a marine, always a marine. I promise you it gets better. When I lost my leg, I thought that was the end of my journey. But really, it was just the beginning of another. I can tell you're a warrior. You always have been and always will be. Now, can I count on you, Marine?"

"I'd do anything for another crack at those barf bag Red Hands. They took my friends from me. They took the Corps from me. I need my payback. Let's take the fight to them," he says.

I step back as the rottweiler stands up proud and tall. "Staff Sergeant Gunner, United States Marine Corps, at your service!" he says.

Then Gunner bites down hard on his leash and rips through it with one jerk of his head.

"You mind freeing an insubordinate Army dog?" I say to Gunner with a smile.

"Roger, Sergeant," he says back to me. "But let's get one thing straight. These Red Hands will be hot on our tails. So we'll have to move swiftly, strategically, and decisively. Which means once we get off this ship, only one of us is calling the shots, and that would be me."

I give Gunner a *north south* and watch as he clamps his teeth around my leash, freeing me. I quickly scan the deck and the situation.

"Those guards are about to switch and leave their post. That'll be our chance. Can you swim?" I ask Gunner.

"For miles on end," he says. "It's about the only thing I'm good at doing these days. Are we—"

"Jumping off the ship?" I say, interrupting him. "It's our only option. The Pawtriots are waiting for us at the Green Dragon Tavern. We need to move fast. Do you know where the tavern is?"

"I could get there blindfolded," Gunner says.

We wait quietly together. Like clockwork, the guards leave the post.

Location: Streets of Boston
Time: 1930 hours

"This way, Rico!" Gunner says, pointing "That's the tavern up ahead."

I follow Gunner through a dirty alley filled with overflowing trash cans, old tires, and broken wooden pallets. It's hard to see through the dark shadows, but that doesn't stop Gunner. I bet he could navigate the city with his eyes closed.

As we get closer to the tavern, I see a green light hanging outside it. Penny is peeking out from behind a dumpster, waving for us to approach her and the rest of the Pawtriots.

"What took you so long?" Penny says to me. She does the "tilt" again as she looks at Gunner, not knowing who he is.

"Long story short," I say, "I got tied up and detained by the Master-at-Arms. But this marine saved me. His name is Staff Sergeant Gunner. He's a tactical asset and has offered to help us. He knows the streets of Boston. And he knows the Red Hands."

"You know the Red Handsss?" asks Smithers.

"Roger, I know them. That's why I'm here, to help take them down. I've got a bone to pick with them, anyway," Gunner says.

"*Oi!*" Brick hollers. "What do these Red Hands want with us?"

"That I'm not sure of. But whatever they want, they usually get. And they're dangerous, so we'll need to be careful," Gunner says.

As everyone is talking, I take a quick mental roll call and realize that all the Pawtriots aren't present and accounted for.

"Penny, where are Jag and Jet?" I ask.

"I sent them to look for you. It was getting late and I was worried. I'm sorry, Rico," Penny says.

"No need for apologies. I put you in charge," I say as I bring Penny in for a hug. "You made a decision, that's all I can ask any leader to do."

"Thanks, Rico," Penny says.

I take a moment to think about what to do next. Every mission has its setbacks, but I can't let that stop me. We've got fellow Pawtriots who are *MIA*—that's Army-talk for "missing in action"— and the Soldier's Creed reminds me, *I will never leave a fallen comrade.* In the Army, we always said, "adapt and overcome." And that's just what I plan on doing.

I turn to Lindy. "I want you to take Daisy, her puppies, Simon, and Franny," I say.

"Tracking. What is our objective?" Lindy says.

"Head south to the TOC as quickly as you can. Your mission is simple: Once you get to DC, I want you to do recon on the Red Hands at the TOC."

"What in the dickens is *recon*?" Daisy asks me.

"It means I want you all to observe what the Red Hands are doing, but from a distance. Tracking?" I say to Daisy, who nods.

"And, Lindy, I repeat: Do not engage," I say. "We'll link up with you as soon as we find Jet and Jag."

"Understood, Rico. Be safe. We'll see you all soon," Lindy says as he motions to Daisy, her pups, Simon, and Franny to follow him.

We all watch as Lindy and his team run off, beginning their trek to Washington, DC.

I turn to the rest of the Pawtriots before me to

give them their orders. "We need to find Jet and Jag. And the sooner, the better. The more time we spend in Boston, the worse things will get back at the TOC. Can I get a north south?"

The Pawtriots all nod.

"Follow me. We'll double back the way we came," I say.

"Negative," says Gunner. "We need some high ground to search for Jet and Jag."

"Where should we go then?" I ask him.

"We'll go to Faneuil Hall Marketplace," Gunner says. "It's a stop on the Freedom Trail, and I know a tall building there. We can climb up the fire escape and use the roof. I'll lead the way."

"*Oi!* Who put you in charge of where we're going?" Brick shouts.

I understand where Brick is coming from. This is our fourth mission as a unit, and at every instance, I've been the leader—the one calling the shots. But a good leader knows when to empower other members of the team to achieve success. We need to find Jet and Jag while avoiding an entire battalion of corgis, so I'll do whatever it takes.

"I did," I tell Brick. "Gunner has full directional authority."

"Well, why didn't you say that?" Brick says with a wink to me.

"Pawtriots, can I get a *Hooah*?" I say to the unit.

"Hooah!" the Pawtriots holler back to me as we make our way through the alley toward Faneuil Hall.

CHAPTER 4
ON THE FREEDOM TRAIL

Location: Faneuil Hall
Time: 1945 hours

As we arrive at Faneuil Hall, I take a quick scan of the area. The cobblestone streets are as old as the buildings. Each street is lined with historic sites and restaurants. And there are plenty of people out and about, which we can use to our advantage.

I call the Pawtriots in for a quick huddle.

"Let's stick together and blend into the crowd. We don't want the Red Hands spotting us while we search for Jet and Jag. Stay close and keep an eye on the Pawtriot in front of you," I say.

"And if you lose contact, just follow the Freedom Trail," says Gunner.

"*Oi!* What's that?" asks Brick.

"A two-point-five-mile-long trail marked throughout Bossston that leads to significant hisstorical locations of the American Revolution," says Smithers.

"Sounds easy enough. Good idea, Gunner," says Penny.

I can tell Gunner is starting to feel like he's part of the team as he finally cracks a smile of confidence.

Time: 2015 hours

We all follow Gunner on the trail, weaving in and out of the foot traffic. Then he leads us down a back alley past trash cans and dumpsters.

"This way," Gunner says, pointing to a fire escape.

He jumps and begins making his way up the fire escape. Brick is next. Then Penny and Smithers. I'm up next, but I can tell that getting up this ladder with my wheel is going to be difficult.

"Come on, Rico!" Penny calls out from the first landing of the fire escape. "You can do it."

I get a running start and make a jump for it,

but I can't get a good grip on the ladder.

Then Gunner leans down and extends his paw. "Grab ahold," he says.

I get another running start and make another jump. I wrap my front paw around a rung of the ladder and let Gunner grab ahold of my wheel.

"Hang tight," Gunner says as he starts pulling me up.

And as I'm hanging there, I feel something whiz past my ears.

Whoosh!

"What was that?" Penny hollers.

"Looksss like an—" Smithers begins to say.

Whoosh!

Another one rushes past me, and then suddenly—

Crack!

Something hits me right on the snout and I can feel the sting of tears in my eyes.

"*Oi!* Rico, hurry up," Brick howls.

I muster all my strength and pull up as hard as I can to get my back legs up on the rung below me for support. I make it to the first landing and pause to catch my breath.

I quickly duck back behind what little cover I have as projectiles whiz over my head. I look down at the ground and notice an intact projectile.

"What is it, Rico?" Penny asks me.

"Acorns," I say, and then—

Whoosh! Whoosh! Crack! Crack!

"It's an ambush!" Gunner hollers. "To the roof!"

I carefully peek out from behind cover. Through my tears, I look down the alley about one hundred yards in the direction from where the acorns are coming. I can see two massive red eyes glowing in the distance. I carefully lift my head up to get a better look, and just as I expose my head—

Whoosh! Whoosh! Crack! Crack!

"Let's move, Sergeant!" howls Gunner.

Time: 2020 hours

We made our way up the fire escape to the roof to get to safety. I huddle the group up close to make an impromptu plan.

"Are you okay, Rico?" Penny asks. "You're bleeding."

"Don't worry; I'll be fine," I tell her. "It just nicked me."

"What was it? And what's going to happen when it's a direct hit?" she asks.

"Acornsss. And I'm ssscared to think about the ssserious damage a direct hit will caussse," Smithers says. "That mussst be the sssecret weapon Jet and Jag were talking about."

"*Oi!* Their secret weapon is acorns?" Brick says with a laugh.

"No," I say, "the acorns are just the ammo."

"Whatever is shooting the acorns is what we need to worry about," Gunner says. "That thing had a cyclic rate of at least a thousand rounds per minute."

"What's a *cyclic rate*?" Penny asks.

"It means how fast a weapon can shoot. But don't worry, Penny. Big weapons tend to miss little targets. We're going to figure this out," I say.

"How? You've already been hit. This could get ugly fast," Penny says. "We split up from Franny, Simon, Lindy, and Daisy, and we don't know where Jet and Jag are."

I'm not sure what exactly we need to do, but I know we need an exit strategy.

"Follow me," I say to the group.

I lead everyone over to the edge of the roof and we all look out to the city below. It's bustling with activity, and I can't see a way out. This old building is much smaller than all of the new ones that surround it.

"Gunner, any thoughts?" I ask.

Gunner surveys the city, his eyes scanning the skyline.

"I don't remember these buildings. I can't see around them. I'm sorry, Rico," says Gunner.

"No time for sorry. Trust your gut and tell us where to go," I say.

"Let's make our way to the Charles River," he says.

"*Oi!*" Brick hollers.

"Brick, quiet," I say. "Gunner has a plan and I want to hear it."

Gunner begins to explain. "Once we get to the river we can—"

"*Oi!*" Brick says again, pointing behind me.

"What is it, Brick?!" I holler back at him.

I turn around to see what he is pointing out.

"Corgis! Twelve o'clock," I howl.

"*Oi!* I was trying to tell you," Brick says.

"What now?" Penny hollers as the corgis begin approaching us. I look around the rooftop. There's nowhere to go.

"Follow me!" Gunner shouts, and begins running to the side of the roof.

We all follow Gunner, running as fast as we can, and then suddenly Gunner jumps from one roof to the next, barely making it to the other side.

"Keep on my tail!" Gunner shouts.

We continue to follow him from rooftop to rooftop, losing more and more corgis with each roof we cross.

Time: 2045 hours

Gunner leads us down a long set of stairs in an abandoned building. Once we make it to the ground level, he turns around, and I can tell he's struggling to breathe as he tries to give out directions.

"Stick to the Freedom Trail and follow me," he says, panting hard.

"Take two mikes, catch your breath," I say to Gunner and the rest of the Pawtriots.

"Negative, Rico. I'm okay. We have to keep moving," says Gunner.

We continue to follow Gunner and the Freedom Trail, making our way through the city streets past beautiful buildings, tall monuments, and statues as we weave in and out of the crowds. Soon the cobblestone streets turn into marshy grass as we make our way closer and closer to the Charles River. I can feel the wind picking up as we get near the water.

Finally, Gunner stops running. We all take a minute to rest.

"*Oi!* I thought you were trying to kill me," Brick says, rolling onto his back in the grass, panting heavily.

"What now?" Penny asks, pointing to the river.

I look out to the river and realize Gunner knows his history. During the American Revolution, colonial soldiers used the river as a natural barrier to keep the British soldiers at bay. We can use the river in the same way and keep the Welsh corgis at a safe distance.

"One if by land," says Gunner.

"Two if by sssea," says Smithers as he motions to the river.

"What's that supposed to mean?" Penny asks.

"During the American Revolution, a colonial patriot from Bossston named Paul Revere helped ssstart an intelligence and alarm sssyssstem to keep watch on the Britisssh Army," Smithers says.

"On the night of hissss hissstoric ride, Revere was tasssked to ride to Lexington, Massachussets, with the newsss that the Britisssh were coming. He usssed lanternsss to relay the newsss to his fellow patriotsss. One lantern meant the Britisssh were arriving by land—"

"And two meant by sea," Gunner finishes.

"But what does that mean for us?" Penny asks.

"You see that boat across the river? We're going to commandeer it and hit the open seas back to DC," I say.

"I'm sick of boats. Big or little! We just got off the sea," Brick hollers.

"Pawtriots, before we get cornered by a battalion of Welsh corgis, let's get our paws wet and make our way to that boat," I say, jumping into the Charles River.

The cold water that surrounds me immediately shocks me. I look across the water and worry that maybe this plan was a bit ill-advised. It's a long way away to the other bank, and the water is choppy. Still, I'm on a mission and have a code to live by—the Soldier's Creed. *I will never quit,*

I remind myself as I begin swimming.

The rest of the Pawtriots jump into the river and follow my lead.

Time: 2115 hours

"We're almost to the other side!" Penny shouts.

"There'd better be some tasty treats on that boat!" Brick hollers.

I want to laugh, but I'm having trouble keeping my head above the water. I was never a great swimmer to begin with, and only having one front paw makes it even harder.

Gunner passes me with ease. And so does Smithers. I'm swimming as hard as I can, but the water is cold, and the current is strong. Water flows into my mouth as I begin to pant.

"Come on, Rico!" Gunner shouts back to me. "Keep pushing."

I feel my wet fur weighing me down even more. I'm panting harder and harder. I can barely breathe. My head is just above the surface.

"Rico!" Penny calls out. "Keep swimming!"

I can see the boat in plain sight. But I'm starting to sink into the cold, dark water. I'm only twenty feet away from the shore, but I realize I'm not going to be able to stay afloat.

I look up one last time to see the Pawtriots safely on the bank of the river. I must be seeing things. It's dark, but I swear I see another dog with them.

A choppy wave rushes over me, and I swallow more water. I'm completely exhausted and begin sinking, and then everything goes black.

CHAPTER 5
OLD DOG, OLD FRIEND

Location: Bank of the Charles River
Time: 2130 hours

I'm dripping wet, looking up at the bright moon, and completely disoriented. Silhouetted by the moon is a mystery dog staring right down at me.

"What happened?" I ask.

"You were drowning. This dog here saved you," Gunner says, pointing to the mystery dog.

"Who are you?" I ask the dog.

"I'm just an old dog looking for an old friend," the mystery dog says, and in an instant I realize who it is.

"Chaps!" I holler as I try to stand up but can't.

"Easy now, Rico. You need to rest," Chaps says, lowering his head next to me so I can get a closer look.

I can barely move my mouth to speak. I feel like I'm seeing a ghost.

"But . . . I saw you . . . and the beast . . . in the sewers. The water was rushing in. There's no way you could've escaped," I say.

"Where there's a will, there's a way," Chaps says with a hearty smile. He extends his paw to help me to my feet. I give him a big hug.

"It's good to see you, too," Chaps says.

I watch as Chaps and Gunner introduce themselves to each other.

"But how did you survive?" I ask.

"I fought like my life depended on it. I gave that foul beast back in DC every ounce of fight I had left in my body. He took my other front leg, but I took him down," says Chaps as he motions down toward his wheel and his prosthetic right leg. "Listen, enough about me. You guys are in serious trouble."

"Tell me about it. We're trying to get back home, but—"

"The Red Hands," Chaps says, cutting me off.

"How'd you know?" I ask him.

"After I managed to escape the sewers and I got fitted with two new legs from an old Army buddy of mine, I didn't know where else to go, so I went back to the Sanctuary. I figured you guys would be there," Chaps says.

"We were in Texas," I tell him.

"Tracking. I knew something wasn't right the moment I got there. So I did some recon. For days and nights I kept watch. Everything was quiet until a few days ago. All I saw were big bulldozers and excavators," Chaps says.

"What for?" Penny asks.

"Well, at first I thought they were going to destroy the place. But then they started digging all around the Sanctuary. Some evil-looking man wearing a white suit and red-rimmed glasses was calling all the shots. He and his two Dobermans barked orders from sunup to sundown," Chaps says.

"That's Mr. Mocoso and his nasty pinschers, Hans and Heinz," I say.

"Did you see Ms. Becca? She's the rightful owner of the Sanctuary. But Mr. Mocoso wants to steal it from her. What happened to her?" I ask him.

"Mr. Mocoso had the Red Hands lock her up in the office," Chaps says.

Things at the TOC are bad, and I wonder if we should have ever left at all. But doubting yourself and your decisions spells trouble for your unit. I have to stay focused.

"So how did you know we'd be in Boston?" I ask Chaps.

"I overheard Mr. Mocoso one night on the phone. He received intel that the Pawtriots were docking in Boston. That's when he called on the Red Hands and ordered that battalion of Welsh corgis to stop you," Chaps says.

"I told you they were bad news," Gunner chimes in.

"Whatever it is they are digging for, they want it for themselves. And they certainly don't want the Pawtriots stopping them," Chaps says. "Oh, and one more thing. Apparently these corgis have some classified secret weapon."

"*Oi!* We know it's some sort of mechanical monster that shoots bloody acorns out of its eyes. It almost put a hole in Rico's head," Brick says.

This is all a lot to take in, but I know I need to stay focused on the mission: Get back home to Washington, DC, and support the rest of the Pawtriots. We can either keep running from the Red Hands and risk being blindsided, or we can bring the fight to them.

"Gunner, any idea where you think the Red Hands will go next?" I ask him.

Gunner takes a moment to think.

"Bunker Hill," he says with confidence.

"Why's that?" I ask.

"Because that's one of the Freedom Trail endpoints. They're trying to match and predict our movements," Gunner says.

"Listen up, Pawtriots. I don't know about you, but I'm tired of running. I'm tired of being on the receiving end of attacks," I say.

"*Oi!* I'm just tired in general!" howls Brick as everyone grins.

"Our home is at stake. What we love is at stake, and it is our duty to protect it. In the Army, I never backed down from a fight, and I don't plan on backing down today. We're going to take the fight to the Red Hands here and now. We're going to take care of business. Can I get a *Hooah*?!"

"*Hooah!*" the Pawtriots holler back at me as we make our way on foot to Bunker Hill.

CHAPTER 6
RED HANDS & WHITE EYES

Location: Bunker Hill
Time: 2200 hours

The moon is high in the night sky. We've been running hard for the last fifteen mikes through the streets of Boston, following Gunner's lead until we arrive at the foot of Bunker Hill, a famous battle site during the American Revolution, where vastly outnumbered Americans faced down the British.

"Welcome to Bunker Hill, Pawtriots," I say.

"So this is where the battle took place?" Penny asks.

"In a way, yesss," Smithers begins, "but technically ssspeaking, the vasssst majority of the battle was fought on Breed'sss Hill, right over there." He points to another hill.

I quickly scan the situation and see the battalion of corgis. They're about three hundred yards away, marching right toward us.

"No time for a history lesson, Smithers! We've got company. Let's move!" I howl.

I look at Gunner and can see he is exhausted.

"Once we get to the top, we can take a quick breather. But we've got to keep moving," I say.

"*Oi!* If we're going to face them, then why not down here?" asks Brick.

"Because up there we have a chance. We need to use the high terrain to our advantage," I say as I point to the top of the hill.

We begin making our way up the hill, and I look back and notice Gunner is struggling to keep up.

"Come on, Gunner. You've got this," I say to give him some motivation. I watch as he picks up his pace and follows my lead.

"*Oi!* Are we there yet?" Brick hollers to me.

"We're almost at the top. Keep moving," I say back.

And just as we reach the top of the hill, I watch as Gunner collapses in exhaustion. We all rush over to help him up.

"I told you, Rico. I'm no good anymore. You're better off without me," says Gunner.

"Negative. Take a few mikes to catch your breath. They don't care if we're tired," I say as I point down to the base of the hill where the corgis are forming up.

As I face down our enemy, I'm reminded of my time in the Army. Even when we were tired, hungry, and thirsty, we still had a job to do.

Suddenly my ears perk up.

"What is it, Rico?" Penny asks me.

"I see Jet and Jag!" I say.

"Oh, thank goodness!" Penny says.

Jet and Jag make their way up the hill to us, and I breathe a sigh of relief.

"What are you doing at the top of Bunker Hill?" Jag calls out, exhausted from sprinting up the hill.

Penny races over to Jet and Jag and gives them a big hug.

"I was worried we'd never see you again," says Penny.

"I'm worried we may never see anyone again if we don't get out of here!" says Jet.

"We're not running anymore. We're going to use the high ground and take the fight to them. If they close in on our position, we'll have to retreat down the other side of the hill," I say.

"Negative, Rico. They've got us surrounded. Check your six," says Jag, pointing behind us.

I turn around and, even through the dark, I can see more corgis—at least ten rows of ten, waiting to strike. In the Army, we were trained to always prepare for the worst but hope for the best. Still, I know hope is not a plan, so I take a quick moment to assess the battlefield and devise a strategy. If we had all the Pawtriots here, we'd stand a chance, but by the looks of it now, we're outnumbered and have nowhere to run. The Red Hands are rapidly closing in on our position from all sides.

"Wait, what in the world is that?" asks Jet, her eyes growing wide.

"That's their secret weapon," I say, looking toward the bottom of the hill at the ten-foot-tall mechanical squirrel.

"These corgis are disciplined, but they're not impenetrable. They march in tight battle formations—the way soldiers in the American Revolution would march into battle," I tell them.

"They'll keep coming in waves," Jag says. "There are hundreds of them."

"*Oi!* We'll never be able to stop them," Brick says. "Especially not with that robot squirrel."

"If we don't take that squirrel out now, we'll just have to deal with it later," Chaps says.

"But how? Even if we destroy the squirrel, there's a thousand Welsh corgis in our way," says Penny.

Penny's right. We're outnumbered. There are at least one hundred twenty-five corgis for every one Pawtriot.

I look around at the Pawtriots and our increasingly dire situation. I think about the colonial soldiers during the American Revolution. They, too, were vastly outnumbered, but they were able to defeat the British because they used their knowledge of the land to their advantage. But I see nothing but trees, grass, dirt . . . and one big steep hill.

Then suddenly I realize, *that's it.*

"Brick! Penny! I need mud balls, now!" I shout as I point to the ground. "That means slobber and dirt!"

"Got it!" Penny says, and she pulls Brick's tongue and lets his drool pour onto the dirt.

And as the Red Hands continue their uphill march toward us, I begin handing out more orders to prepare for this attack.

"Jet and Jag: I need you here and here," I say, directing them to assume positions about three feet apart.

"Smithers, I want you to wrap around them," I say, pointing to Jet and Jag.

"Why?" Smithers asks.

"Because you'll be the slingshot for the mud balls," I say.

Smithers wraps his head around Jag and his tail around Jet. Then I look over at Brick and Penny and see they've already got dozens of mud balls ready to go.

"Hurry up, Army! They're closing in!" Gunner says.

The Red Hands at our front are only about twenty-five yards away. Now is my time to get into position. I roll onto my back and put my wheel leg in the air.

I take a moment to look up from my back and check the situation. It's dire, but as I look at all the Pawtriots, I can't help but feel proud. They're ready and brave. They show no fear.

"Brick, you're in charge of launching. Penny, keep the mud balls coming," I say.

"I'm on it," Brick says. Then he places a mud ball on my wheel and moves into position behind me.

I look over and see Gunner standing tall at the top of the hill. He's growling and ready to fight. He may be old, but he's got a lot of good fight still left in him.

"Come on, Red Hands! I'll take you all on myself!" Gunner hollers.

I admire Gunner's tenacity, but no battle is won by a single soldier. It's a team effort, and I need to remind him about that.

"Gunner, focus!" I howl at him. "Once I start firing, I need you to be my eyes. Get a good position for a vantage point."

"Oorah!" Gunner shouts, racing past me as he climbs onto a tree perch overlooking the battlefield.

I peek back up and see the Red Hands are only about fifteen yards away.

"Oi! Should I shoot?" Brick asks as he slowly pulls Smithers back over my wheel like a slingshot.

"Negative!" I howl.

I know Brick is anxious to begin, especially with the Red Hands approaching. But we need to draw them in as close as possible before we start launching mud balls. The hill is steeper closer to the top. If we time this right, we should be able to throw them off balance. This is just how the colonials won the American Revolution: using the terrain to their advantage. I plan to do the exact same thing.

"Don't fire until you see the whites of their eyes," I holler to my unit.

"Rico, they're closing in fast," Chaps howls back.

"Steady," I say.

"*Oi!* Rico, come on," Brick hollers.

"Steady," I say, peeking down the hill.

And just when I can clearly see the tops of the first row of corgis' heads, I know this is our signal.

"*Fire!*" I howl.

The mud balls fly through the air, and I look up at Gunner for guidance.

"Rico, adjust fire. Aim ten feet left!" shouts Gunner as acorns begin to pummel him.

I angle my body to the left as Brick keeps firing mud balls.

"Direct hit!" Gunner howls from the tree. "Keep firing!"

"Fire at will!" I call out to the Pawtriots. I watch as Brick sends mud ball after mud ball down the hill, smashing hard into the rows of Red Hands. I can hear them howl as they tumble down the steep hill.

"*Oi!* It's working. They're dropping like flies!" Brick shouts as he keeps on firing mud balls. But they are retaliating, and I can feel acorns rushing past us.

The corgis are closing in on all sides, and I feel like time is running out. We're fighting hard, but there are just too many of them.

"We need to take out that squirrel! Use this," Penny shouts as she positions a massive mud ball on top of my wheel. It's so heavy, my leg starts to buckle.

"Fire!" I howl.

I hop to my feet and watch as the massive mud ball hurtles toward the robotic squirrel and then—

Wham!

"Direct hit!" Penny hollers. We all watch in awe as the robot squirrel quickly goes haywire and begins twitching. Smoke billows from its ear and eye sockets until it explodes.

"Rico, we need to move!" shouts Gunner as he jumps down from the tree. "They're closing in on our six! Follow me!" He charges down the hill with reckless abandon, barreling into corgis and sending them hard into the ground.

"He's clearing a path. Follow Gunner!" I shout.

The Pawtriots and I begin making our way down the front of Bunker Hill, using Gunner as our lead dog. I'm not sure where he's leading us, but I have full trust he'll get us out of here safely.

My heart is racing as fast as my wheel is turning. I watch as my unit and Gunner make their way down the hill, skillfully avoiding the fallen Red Hands. Every adventure the Pawtriots and I get into is exhilarating and reminds me of being right back in the Army and not knowing where you're going next, but knowing it will be even better than the last place.

Time: 2300 hours

We've been running for the last thirty minutes, making our way through the streets of Boston, back past Faneuil Hall, and finally stopping at a train station. We all take a minute to catch our breath and rest on the platform.

"What are we doing here?" I ask Gunner.

"Well, you guys need to get back to DC. I'll sneak you onto the back of a cargo train," Gunner says. "This train will get you where you need to go."

The Pawtriots file onto the train. I begin

to make my way on and see that Gunner is still standing on the platform.

"Are you coming with us?" I ask him.

"Negative, Rico. I've done all I can. I'm old and tired. And Boston is my home," Gunner says.

I take a good look at him. I'm reminded of myself when I first met Penny and Ms. Becca, and they brought me into the Sanctuary, into their home.

"Home is where the heart is," I say to Gunner, "and you belong in a unit, *our* unit. You were born to be a Pawtriot!"

"You know, for an insubordinate Army dog, I like you," Gunner says with a smile as he makes his way onto the train with the rest of us.

CHAPTER 7
TIC-TOC

Location: Cargo Train, Washington, DC
Date: 21MAR21
Time: 0530 hours

We've been resting in the cargo train for about six hours now. We're sharing a car with a bunch of police horses. They're awfully nice, but they're also in dire need of a shower.

"*Oi!* Who picked this manure mobile?" Brick asks.

"Would you prefer I found us a car full of corgis and a robotic squirrel?" Gunner says with a smile.

Meanwhile, I've been sticking my head through

the slats in the side of the train car to get some fresh air. I'm watching the trees go by as we make our way down the Atlantic coast.

When the train begins to slow down, I know we're getting close to Washington, DC.

"On your feet, Pawtriots," I say. "The walk from Union Station to the TOC is about thirty miles. Let's get to it."

It feels good to almost be back home where my journey began.

Location: Outskirts of the TOC
Time: 0830 hours

"*Oi!* I can't wait to get into my bed—my *own* bed!" Brick calls out as we get closer to the TOC.

"And I can't wait to see Ms. Becca!" Penny says.

We're just about back home, and I feel the same way. It's been a long time since I was last here. We've been through thick and thin together and it's so nice be in a familiar place. Still, I know we're not in the clear just yet.

Chaps pulls me in close and whispers, "Rico,

this isn't going to be the homecoming your friends are hoping for."

"I'm tracking. Thanks, Chaps," I say. "We couldn't have made it this far without you."

We're just about there but, before we go any farther, I pause to address the group.

"Listen up, Pawtriots. When we get back to the TOC, we're still on a mission. Morgan and Sawyer are in trouble, Ms. Becca is being held captive, and we still need to link up with Lindy, Franny, Simon, and Daisy and her pups," I say.

Chaps chimes in. "And based on my recon, Mr. Mocoso, Hans, and Heinz will be waiting for us. We need to proceed with caution," he says.

"Tracking. Let's move out," I say to the group, and they follow my lead.

And as we turn the corner, I set my eyes on the TOC.

The TOC is a hotbed of activity. Dump trucks, excavators, and bulldozers have dug a hole about thirty feet deep into the ground. I scan the area and see several men in black suits with the Red Hands insignia on their lapels. Some use shovels to dig, while others haul bags out of the hole and load them into a twenty-foot-long steel container. There's even a helicopter hovering right above the TOC.

"What are they digging for?" Penny whispers to me.

"Looksss ssshiny," Smithers says.

"He's right. It looks like gold," I say to her. I continue to look around for Lindy. He's in charge of Franny, Simon, and Daisy and her pups. I know they're in safe hands with Lindy, but they should be here already, so I'm starting to get worried.

Suddenly a glimmer of light shines in my eyes. I put up my paw to block the light and lower my head to avoid the glare.

And that's when I see Morgan and Sawyer in the alley across the way, hiding behind a dumpster with all of the other animals from the TOC.

Morgan's reflecting the light with a piece of metal, and Sawyer is waving for us to join them.

"Are they friends of yours?" asks Gunner.

"Sure are," I say. "Come on. Let's go link up with them."

Location: Alleyway Outside the TOC
Time: 0900 hours

We make it over to Morgan and Sawyer's location and take cover behind the dumpster. Morgan and Sawyer salute me and then realize Chaps is with us. They blow past me and jump onto Chaps and give him a big hug.

"It's so good to see you guys," says Chaps.

"I see you made some new friends," says Morgan as she motions to Gunner, Jet, and Jag.

"They're Pawtriots now, too. We can do proper introductions later," I say.

"We're glad you're here. Things are pretty bad. We could use the reinforcements," Morgan says.

"Have you seen Sawyer?" I ask. "He was supposed to be here with the other Pawtriots."

"Roger. She said you'd be right behind them. They're in position just waiting for the order to attack," says Morgan. "Look over there. Three o'clock."

I turn to my right and see Franny, Lindy, Daisy, her puppies, and Simon holed up behind a parked car down the street. I give Lindy a *paws*-up.

It feels good knowing that we're going into battle with all the Pawtriots.

CHAPTER 8
BATTLE FOR THE TOC

Location: Alleyway Outside the TOC
Time: 0930 hours

My plan is straightforward. We're going to charge toward the TOC with the speed and fury of a buffalo stampede.

"Pawtriots, you ready?" I ask.

"We're ready," says Penny.

But as I look into the eyes of the Pawtriots, I can tell they're scared and I don't blame them, because I am, too.

"Pawtriots. Listen up and listen good. This is more than just the TOC or the Sanctuary. We are going to take the fight to Mr. Mocoso, Hans, Heinz, and the Red Hands, and we're going to take it to them hard. They came to take gold. But we're fighting for more than that. We're fighting for our home!" I howl.

As I stand before the Pawtriots, Gunner saunters up beside me and leans in close.

"Hey, Rico, thanks a lot," whispers Gunner.

"For what?" I whisper back.

"Making me realize that I've still got some fight left in me," says Gunner.

"Hooah!" yell the Pawtriots in unison as we all march forward.

CHAPTER 9
MISSION ACCOMPLISHED

```
Location: The TOC
Date: 4MAY21
Time: 1100
```

It's been seven weeks since the battle for the TOC. And it had been months since all the Pawtriots had been together. But it feels good to be back home where it all started.

During the battle, we were tired and outnumbered, but we took back the TOC and saved the Sanctuary . . . again. We fought hard against the forces of evil and showed bravery at every turn.

The Red Hands, Mr. Mocoso, Hans, and Heinz met us with fury. But they fought for greed and power. The Pawtriots fought for our home, our freedom, and for one another.

And just as quickly as the battle had begun, it was over.

Still, Mr. Mocoso, his nasty pinschers, and a few Red Hands managed to escape. They had already loaded all the gold buried beneath the TOC into the shipping container. All they needed was a way out.

Mr. Mocoso scurried onto the shipping container as a transport helicopter hovered above. While some of the Red Hands secured the container to the helicopter with chains, Hans and Heinz couldn't help but reveal their diabolical plan.

"You fools really think you won, don't you?" Hans snickered as he reluctantly backed away from the battlefield in retreat. "This is just the beginning!"

Then Heinz called out, "We never wanted this stinking place. We wanted the gold! Mr. Mocoso has far bigger plans. And if I were you, Rico, I'd be very worried!"

As I watched them slip away, I realized that this wouldn't be the last time we would cross paths. We had won the battle, but the war against evil had just begun.

Hans and Heinz even sent us a written message last week, taunting us more.

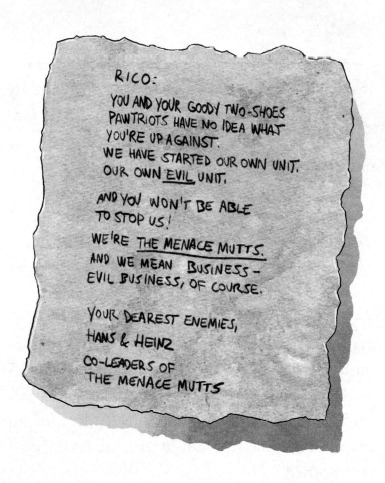

RICO:

YOU AND YOUR GOODY TWO-SHOES PAWTRIOTS HAVE NO IDEA WHAT YOU'RE UP AGAINST.
WE HAVE STARTED OUR OWN UNIT. OUR OWN EVIL UNIT.

AND YOU WON'T BE ABLE TO STOP US!

WE'RE THE MENACE MUTTS.
AND WE MEAN BUSINESS — EVIL BUSINESS, OF COURSE.

YOUR DEAREST ENEMIES,

HANS & HEINZ

CO-LEADERS OF
THE MENACE MUTTS

After the battle for the TOC, it took us a few weeks to get everything back up and running, but we are better for it. And now that we've recruited Pawtriots from each branch of the Armed Forces—Army, Navy, Air Force, Coast Guard, and

Marines—I gave them all tasks and purpose. If we're going to continue fighting evil, we must be well organized.

Sergeant Rico: .... Commander

Penny and Brick: .... Recruitment

Franny, Smithers, Morgan, Sawyer: .... Tactics Instructors

Chaps: .... Drill Instructor

Daisy: .... Maneuvers Instructor

Simon: .... Signals Instructor

Lindy: .... Air Force Instructor

Jet: .... Coast Guard Instructor

Jag: .... Navy Instructor

Gunner: ..... Marine Instructor

The Pawtriots were already a household name after we saved the Sanctuary the first time around. We were getting fan mail every week, but once word spread about all the adventures we had just been on, fan mail started arriving daily. Animals from across the country had heard the stories about all the animals we saved and all the beasts, spiders, krakens, and robots we defeated.

I love reading every letter. Each one reminds me of the Pawtriots' true purpose: to help those in need.

I write every animal back so they know that the Pawtriots are ready, willing, and able to help. I tell everyone that no matter how long it takes or how far we must go, we won't ever give up until our mission is complete.

And I always sign my letters the same:

Stay strong. The Pawtriots are on the way!

—Sergeant "Rico" Ricochet

GLOSSARY OF ARMY-TALK

In each book of the Pawtriot Dogs series, author and former Army Captain Samuel P. Fortsch incorporates words and phrases he and his fellow soldiers used in the Army. The following is a list of some of those sayings, as reported directly from Fortsch himself. These definitions are not official; rather, they show the way actual soldiers speak on and off the battlefield.

- **Affirmative** — Another way to say "yes" or "correct"

- **AO** — Abbreviation of "Area of Operations." This is a designated area where a unit will be conducting combat operations.

- **Brig** — A holding cell

- **Camo-up** — To apply camouflage

- **Chow** — Food

- **Class 1** — The class of supply regarding your unit's current levels of food and water

- **Cyclic Rate** — How fast a weapon can shoot

- **Debrief** — To quickly explain a situation to someone

- **Double-time** — To move twice as fast, or simply, "hurry up"

- **Exfil** — To withdraw from or leave a location

- **Eyes on** — Say this when you want to know whether someone can see the thing you are pointing to. For instance, "Do you have eyes on the ship in the distance?"

- **Flank** — The sides of a military formation

- **Hard-liner** — Someone who sticks closely to the rules

- **Hard time** — A deadline

- **High-speed** — Really cool equipment or a highly skilled soldier

- **Hooah** — This is the Army's rallying cry. Soldiers use it in many instances, but most commonly as a way to say, "Let's go!"

- **Intel** — Short for "intelligence," meaning any useful information

- **King of Battle** — Nickname for the Field Artillery

- **Klick** — Short for "one kilometer"

- **LDA** — Abbreviation of "Linear Danger Area." This is a long, narrow open area that is risky to cross, as you and your unit will be exposed to the enemy.

- **Lock it up** — To be quiet

- **MIA** — Abbreviation of "Missing in Action." Say this when somebody is unaccounted for.

- **Mikes** — Minutes

- **Move out** — Start walking or running to another location

- **MRE** — Abbreviation for "Meal, Ready to Eat." These are individual rations for service members when they are on the go and don't have access to a proper food facility.

- **Negative** — Another way to say "no"

- **Noise and light discipline** — Short way to say, "No loud noises or bright lights, as they may give away our position."

- **North South** — To nod your head up and down, as in the direction of north to south. This motion signals "yes" or means you understand what is being asked of you.

- **NVG** — Abbreviation of "Night Vision Goggles," which soldiers use to see in the dark

- **On Me** — Short for "huddle up next to me"

- **OPSEC** — Abbreviation of "Operations Security," meaning it's not safe to tell people you don't know the details of your mission

- **Outside the wire** — To leave your base and go out on a mission

- **PT** — Abbreviation for "Physical Training," like running, push-ups, and sit-ups

- **Pop Smoke** — To leave or retreat an area quickly

- **R&R** — Abbreviation for "Rest and Relaxation," because even soldiers need to rest

- **Recon** — To explore and scout an area to gain information about any activity

- **Roger that** — To confirm that a message has been received. In short, it means "I understand."

- **RP1** — Rally Point #1, the first place where troops meet during a mission

- **RTB** — Abbreviation of "Return to Base," meaning "time to go home"

- **SitRep** — Abbreviation of "Situation Report." This is a written document containing all the details—the who, what, where, when, why—of the mission.

- **Ten toes up** — To be asleep on your back

- **Three points of contact** — To make sure you have at least two hands and one foot or two feet and one hand in contact with whatever obstacle you're moving up or down on. This increases your chances of safely navigating the obstacle.

- **TOC** — Abbreviation for "Tactical Operations Center." This is a place where battlefield operations are tracked and coordinated.

- **Tracking** — Short for "I understand"

AN INTERVIEW WITH AUTHOR SAMUEL P. FORTSCH

What inspired you to write this series?

I was inspired to write this series after my oldest son, Samuel, asked me what being in the Army was like. At the time, he was only five years old, and I didn't have a good answer for him. I decided that I would create a fictional world replacing soldiers with animals so that he might better understand. It turns out he really loved the world and the stories, so I kept writing.

Would you say writing is easy for you?

Writing is easy . . . if you have a plan. So, before I start writing, I spend a lot of time working out the characters, the plot, and the purpose of the story. Then I start to fill in the details. And that's the fun part!

So, what was being in the Army like?

The Army was like being a part of a team where each soldier, regardless of rank, works together toward a common goal.

In the Army, if you're not deployed overseas, the average day consists of PT (Physical Training), which starts at 0630. After PT, there are various types of training exercises, which include small arms weapons training, troop movement and tactics, land navigation, and first aid training. All of this training prepares you for deployment.

What are some values you learned during your service? Do you still use those values today?

LDRSHIP is a great Army acronym that stands for Loyalty, Duty, Respect, Selfless Service, Honor, Integrity, and Personal Courage. Those values are instilled in you from day one in the Army, and they have stuck with me until this day.

What are some of your best memories from during your service? What will you miss about being in the Army?

The best memories I have of my time in the Army are about all the different people I met along the way. The Army is one of the most diverse organizations in the world, and it allowed me to travel the world and meet people from all walks of life. I will miss the camaraderie and adventures that came with it.

What do you want readers to take away from Pawtriot Dogs?

I hope that once readers finish the series, they will realize that most challenges they may face can often be overcome with hard work, motivation, and the support of friends.

In the series, the main character, Rico, looks toward his handler, Kris, for inspiration. Could you tell us more about the real-life Kris?

Kristen Marie Griest is one of the first two women to graduate from the US Army Ranger School. I served with "Kris" in Afghanistan on my second deployment with the 101st. To me, she personified what it meant to be a soldier in the US Army. In the series, Rico often turns to the fictional version of Kris. In my life, I turned to the real one.